# NICK JR. The BACKYARDIGANS™

# Secret Agents

adapted by Wendy Wax

based on the original teleplay "Secret Mission"
by McPaul Smith

illustrated by Zina Saunders

SIMON SPOTLIGHT / NICK JR.

New York    London    Toronto    Sydney

**visit us at www.abdopublishing.com**

Reinforced library bound edition published in 2007 by Spotlight, a division of ABDO Publishing Group, Edina, Minnesota. Published by agreement with Simon Spotlight, Simon & Schuster Children's Publishing Division.

Text by Wendy Wax based on the original teleplay "Secret Mission" by McPaul Smith. Illustrations by Zina Saunders. Based on the TV series *Nick Jr. The Backyardigans*™ as seen on Nick Jr.® Reprinted with permission of Simon Spotlight, Simon & Schuster Children's Publishing Division. All rights reserved.

An Imprint of Simon & Schuster Children's Publishing Division
1230 Avenue of the Americas, New York, New York 10020

Simon Spotlight

**Library of Congress Cataloging-In-Publication Data**

This title was previously cataloged with the following information:

Wax, Wendy

Secret agents / adapted by Wendy Wax ; illustrated by Zina Saunders.

    p. cm. (The Backyardigans ; bk. #3)

ISBN 1-1169-1226-6 (paperback)

Summary: The Backyardigans imagine that they are secret agents who get into sticky situations when they sneak into the Treasure Museum.

[1. Animals--Juvenile fiction. 2. Spies--Juvenile fiction. 3. Museums--Juvenile fiction. 4. Imagination--Juvenile fiction. 5. Adventure and adventurers--Juvenile fiction. 6. Animals--Fiction. 7. Spies--Fiction. 8. Museums--Fiction. 9. Imagination--Fiction. 10. Adventure and adventurers--Fiction.] I. Saunders, Zina, ill. II. Title. III. Series.

[E]--dc22
                                    2006296610

ISBN-13: 978-1-59961-161-7 (reinforced library bound edition)
ISBN-10: 1-59961-161-9 (reinforced library bound edition)

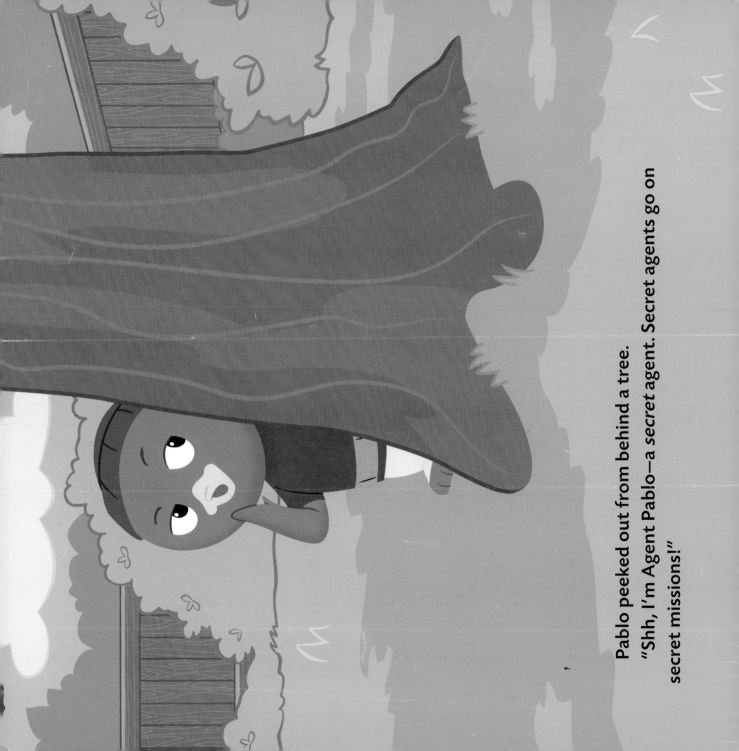

Pablo peeked out from behind a tree.
"Shh, I'm Agent Pablo—a secret agent. Secret agents go on secret missions!"

Tyrone crept out from behind a bush. "I'm Agent Tyrone!" he said.
"All clear, Agent Pablo?"
"All clear, Agent Tyrone!" said Pablo.

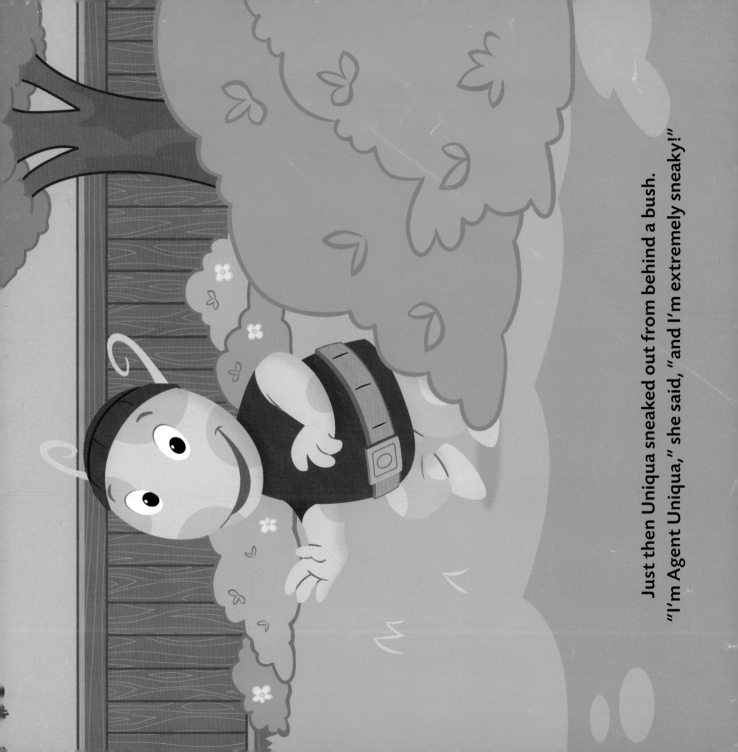

Just then Uniqua sneaked out from behind a bush.
"I'm Agent Uniqua," she said, "and I'm extremely sneaky!"

"What is our secret mission, Agent Pablo?" asked Tyrone. Pablo held up a box with a bone inside it. "We need to sneak into the Treasure Museum to return this mystery bone to its secret owner," he said.

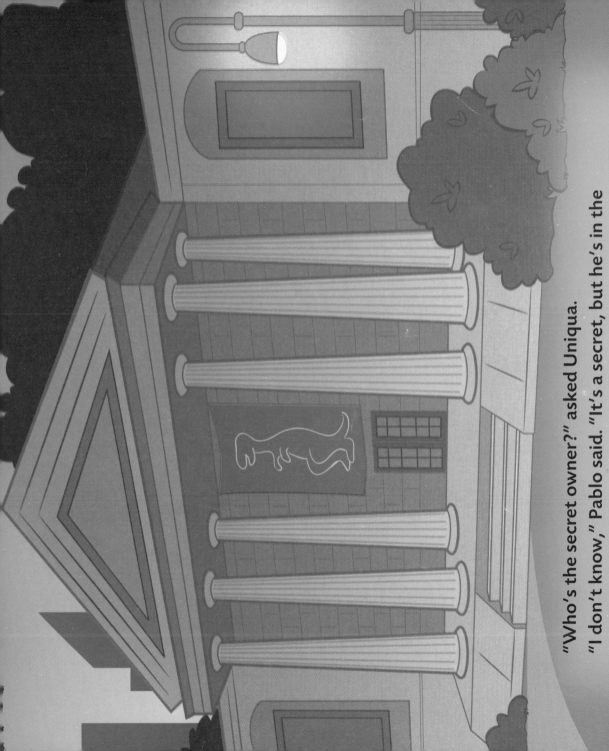

"Who's the secret owner?" asked Uniqua.

"I don't know," Pablo said. "It's a secret, but he's in the Treasure Museum."

"But the Treasure Museum has alarms and booby traps!" said Tyrone.

"Secret agents can always find a way to sneak in," said Uniqua.

Outside the Treasure Museum, Pablo showed the other agents his spy gadget. It was small with lots of top-secret buttons. Uniqua had brought a spy power rope to help them in tough situations. Tyrone had brought a bottle of maple syrup.

"Maple syrup!" said Pablo and Uniqua. "What's that for?"

"It's spy maple syrup," said Tyrone. "In case we need something sticky."

"Let's go," said Uniqua. "Secret agents never just go in. They *sneak in!*" said Pablo. He used his spy gadget to open a secret trap door at their feet.

"How will we get down there?" asked Tyrone.

"No problem! With my spy power rope!" said Uniqua. "Grab on, agents! We're going down!"

The secret agents found themselve in the Hall of Precious Jewels. "Rubies, emeralds, and pearls!" sai Tyrone. "These certainly are precious jewels."

"Watch out for alarms and booby traps in here," said Pablo.

"Look! This must be the biggest diamond in the world," Uniqua exclaimed, turning to her friends. But in her excitement, she bumped into the stand that held the huge diamond.

"Watch out!" Pablo cried as the diamond fell.

Tyrone caught the
diamond—just as a cage
fell down from the ceiling.
Clank!

"Oh, no!" cried Uniqua.
"A booby trap!"

"We're trapped!" cried
Pablo, starting to panic.

"Uh-oh! Secret agents
should never get trapped.
But we're trapped.
Uh-oh . . ."

"Pablo!" said Uniqua. "Calm down. We have to be cool and think."

"We could try my spy maple syrup," suggested Tyrone.

"Nah," said Uniqua and Pablo.

"Maybe if we put the diamond back, the cage will go up," said Uniqua. Pablo pressed a button on his spy gadget. A mechanical arm with a claw grabbed the diamond and returned it to its base—and the cage began to rise.

The agents came to a doorway. Three laser beams blocked their way.

"If we touch the laser beams, we'll set off an alarm!" warned Pablo.

"But how do we get past them?" asked Tyrone.

"We've got to do the limbo under the beams," said Pablo.

After they carefully went under the laser beams, the secret agents came upon the Gargantuan Gallery.

"How will we find the secret owner of the mystery bone?" Uniqua asked.

Just then she tripped over a dinosaur's foot. It was missing a baby toe.

"You found him!" said Pablo. "The mystery bone is the dinosaur's toe!"

"We need something sticky to attach the toe to the foot," said Uniqua.

"I *knew* my spy maple syrup would come in handy," said Tyrone. He stuck the bone in place. "Mission accomplished!"

"Let's get out of here!" said Tyrone.

Uniqua shot the spy power rope up through the skylight.

"Grab hold, agents!" she said. "Going up!"

"That was quite a mysterious adventure!"
said Tyrone.
"And very sneaky," said Uniqua.
"Now let's have a snack at my house!"
So off they all went for a secret agent snack.